KADDISH FOR GRANDPA
in Jesus' name
amen

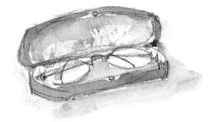

❦

To my daughter, Zoey,
and in memory of her Grandpa Art
—J. H.

For Ben, Alex, Torrey, Adam, and Emma
—C. S.

Atheneum Books for Young Readers
An imprint of Simon & Schuster Children's Publishing Division
1230 Avenue of the Americas
New York, New York 10020
Text copyright © 2004 by James Howe
Illustrations copyright © 2004 by Catherine Stock
Book design by Ann Bobco and Sonia Chaghatzbanian
The text of this book is set in Garamond.
The illustrations are rendered in watercolors.
Manufactured in China
First Edition
2 4 6 8 10 9 7 5 3 1
Library of Congress Cataloging-in-Publication Data
Howe, James.
Kaddish for Grandpa in Jesus' name amen / James Howe ; illustrated by Catherine Stock.—1st ed.
p.   cm.
Summary: Five-year-old Emily tries to understand her grandfather's death by exploring the Christian and Jewish rituals that
her family practices during and after his funeral.
ISBN 0-689-80185-8
[1. Funeral rites and ceremonies—Fiction. 2. Death—Religious aspects—Fiction. 3. Grandfathers—Fiction.
4. Judaism—Fiction. 5. Christianity—Fiction.] I. Stock, Catherine, ill. II. Title.
PZ7 .H83727 Kad 2004
[Fic]—dc21   2002011569

JAMES HOWE • CATHERINE STOCK

KADDISH FOR GRANDPA
in Jesus' name
amen

Atheneum Books for Young Readers
New York London Toronto Sydney

When I was new,
my grandpa was very old.
He held me on his knees
and gazed into my eyes.

When I was two, he sang songs to me.

When I was four, he read me stories. Sometimes he missed the words because he didn't have his glasses.

"Here they are!" I would say.

Grandpa would give me a big squeeze. "What would I do without you?" he would ask me. And then he would say, "Well, I guess we'd better go back and find all those lost words!" And he would turn back to the beginning of the story and start reading all over again.

When I was five, my grandpa died. Daddy came to tell me while I was taking my bath. After he told me, he moved the washcloth up and down on my back while he hummed a song. It was one of the songs Grandpa used to sing to me. My daddy's voice sounded sad.

Daddy went away for a couple of days to be with my grandma and my uncles to make plans for Grandpa's funeral. I asked Mommy what a funeral was.

"It's a time for the people who love someone who has died to come together and remember that person in a special way," she said. "It's a time for singing songs and telling stories."

I liked that part. I told her, "That's what Grandpa used to do with me."

She told me that even though we were Jewish, the funeral would be Christian because that's what Daddy's family is. Daddy chose to be Jewish when he was a grown-up. Mommy was born Jewish, like me.

I didn't understand that part. If a funeral was a time for singing songs and telling stories, why did it have to be Christian or Jewish?

After school ended on Friday, Mommy and I flew to where Grandma lives. Daddy was happy to see me. He didn't look sad anymore.

He even laughed with my uncles and aunts and
cousins that night at Grandma's house.

When I was eating a cookie after dinner, I sat down in Grandpa's chair. My fingers felt something in the crack beside the cushion. It was the case for Grandpa's glasses. I started to go and give it to him. And then I remembered he wasn't there.

In the morning while we were getting dressed, Daddy said, "There will be flowers for Grandpa at the funeral. Would you like to bring flowers, too?"

I said I would. I drew a picture of flowers and I wrote on it, FOR GRANDPA. I LOVE YOU. EMILY.

The funeral was in a church. I had never been in a church before. I liked all the colors in the windows, but there were too many people. I held tight to Daddy's hand.

In the front of the church was
a long box that Daddy said had
Grandpa's body in it. Daddy
explained that when Grandpa died
he had left his body behind because
it had grown old and worn out.

"It's Grandpa's memory that
lives on," Daddy said. "Here."
He touched his heart. "And here."
He touched mine.

Then Daddy took my hand and
we walked up to the box at the
front of the church, and I put my
picture of flowers right on top of it.

When we sat down next to Mommy, the music started. There were songs that were pretty, but I didn't know the words. Songs about angels and joyful, joyful we adore thee. And prayers that ended in Jesus' name amen.

People stood up and told stories about Grandpa. Sometimes people laughed and sometimes people cried. Mommy cried and Daddy cried, too. I didn't like that part.

The day after the funeral, we said goodbye to Grandma and to my uncles and aunts and cousins, and we flew back home.

Daddy said he wanted to remember Grandpa in a Jewish way, too. And so he lit a special candle that burned through the night, and for a few evenings people came to our house bringing cakes and cookies. They looked at the picture of Grandpa that Daddy had put on the mantel over the fireplace and listened to the stories that he and Mommy told.

Each evening the rabbi came and led everyone in a special prayer called the Kaddish. The words were in Hebrew, and even though I didn't know what they meant, I liked the sound of them because they reminded me of being in temple.

And then one night, after the people had stopped coming and the candle was no longer burning, Daddy was putting me to bed when his fingers felt something under my pillow.

"What's this?" he asked.

I pulled it out to show him. It was the case for Grandpa's glasses. "Grandma gave it to me," I told him. "She said I was always the best one at helping Grandpa find his glasses. I touch it every night before I go to sleep."

"To remember Grandpa," Daddy said in a soft voice.

I nodded, and Daddy kissed me on the forehead.

After Daddy left my room, I touched Grandpa's glasses case to my heart. I closed my eyes and pictured his wrinkled face. I could almost hear him singing to me.

"Good night, Grandpa," I said.

And then I slid the glasses case under my pillow and kept my hand on it while I fell asleep.

It wasn't the Christian way and it wasn't the Jewish way. It was just my way. My Kaddish for Grandpa in Jesus' name amen.